Hello, Crow

STORY BY **Jeff Daniel Marion**

ILLUSTRATED BY **Leslie Bowman**

ORCHARD BOOKS   NEW YORK

Orchard Books, 95 Madison Avenue, New York, NY 10016

Manufactured in the United States of America. Printed by Barton Press, Inc. Bound by Horowitz/Rae. Book design by Mina Greenstein. The text of this book is set in 18 point Usherwood Medium. The illustrations are colored pencil, reproduced in full color.
10 9 8 7 6 5 4 3 2 1

Library of Congress Cataloging-in-Publication Data
Marion, Jeff Daniel, date.   Hello, Crow / story by Jeff Daniel Marion ; illustrated by Leslie Bowman.   p.   cm.   Summary:
Reminiscences of a boy about his brief relationship with a crow that lived for a while in the well house.
ISBN 0-531-05975-8.   ISBN 0-531-08575-9 (lib. bdg.)   1. Crows—Juvenile fiction.   [1. Crows—Fiction.]   I. Bowman, Leslie W., ill.
II. Title.   PZ10.3.M3223He   1992   [E]—dc20   91-18561

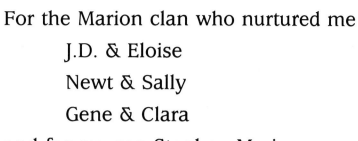

For the Marion clan who nurtured me
  J.D. & Eloise
  Newt & Sally
  Gene & Clara
and for my son Stephen Marion
and my daughter Rachel Marion Franklin
  storytellers all
     —J.D.M.

To my father, Richard W. Bowman
    —L.B.

Years ago when I was a boy in the mountains,
I went daily to draw water in the cool,
latticed shade of the well house.

For my amusement, Grandfather had brought home
a nestling, housed him on a perch.

Each day I went about my chores,
a single greeting always offered:
"Hello, Crow."

What Grandmother remembered was theft
and the many secret pockets to hide his plunder:

three silver teaspoons washed out of the gutter
in the first April downpour;

on a December morning, seven dimes
gleaming from the forks of the pear tree;

and day after day, here and there,
startling revelations—

an earring dangling
from a dogwood branch,

and in the milk-glass cookie jar,
far beyond reach on the top shelf of the cupboard,

a single black feather.

On a gray November morning,
stooped to my task of drawing water,
I forgot my greeting.

Behind me, Crow sat hunched in a corner.

Raindrops pinged on the tin roof.

In that moment I swear I heard
in a distinct crow voice: Hello.

Crow never spoke again
although I always expected him to.

Daily I kept up my greetings,
but he only cocked his head to eye the gleam
of the well bucket's bail.

Then one morning he was gone.

"Flown the coop," my grandfather said.

"He'll come back," I said.

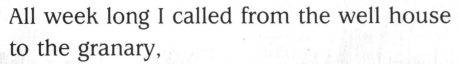

All week long I called from the well house
to the granary,

from the pasture to the pond;
all over the farm I called,
"Hello, Crow. Hello."

Two years after his disappearance
I remember a traveling circus
and a little sideshow
with an animal trainer
on whose shoulder perched a talking crow.

Hello, Crow.

Today I study the sky and still wonder

each time I see those sooty flecks
rising in a faraway field.

Then I lift my hand as if to call:

Hello, Crow.

Hello.